BRIDGE OVER SHIFTING WATER

A PARANORMAL WOMEN'S FICTION SHORT

MURKY MIDLIFE WATERS
BOOK THREE

JB LASSALLE

MIGHTY OAK
PUBLISHING SERVICES

CHAPTER 1

 was in the groove until that massive demon bug launched its attack.

My freestyle was on point. My backstroke was a thing of beauty. My butterfly … needed work. I'd hit my groove. I had no idea what I actually looked like, but in my mind, I sliced through the water like an athlete, sleek and steady.

Sure, my goggles were too tight, and they leaked in the corner until my eyes burned, but surely the pros struggled the same way.

Then, that nasty brown carapaced monster dashed across the pool with an Olympic level of speed. Tiny claws snapped open and closed, ready to clamp down on whatever part of my body it reached first. Beady, soulless eyes glared.

I screamed underwater, the sound not at all melodic or alluring like a siren's should be and splashed with all my might to force the nasty critter in the opposite direction. Stumbling against the waves I'd created, I made a half-swimming, half-running escape to the pool ladder.

I crawled out, my heart pounding into my ears, and searched out the monster hell-bent on my death. I found it gliding through the center of the pool, unperturbed by my actions. It was no more than 3 inches long, grossly fat, with tiny pincers and four crab-like legs. A dark shell covered it. Long antennae tasted the water, searching for prey.

I let out a full body shudder and wrapped my towel around myself. The few times I'd swam as a mermaid in the bay, the creatures who called it home had done little more than eye me curiously or shift away as my tail flapped. I'd assumed they understood I was somehow like them. Part of their world.

But in the pool, I always seemed to forget that I was part-mermaid and flopped about like a toddler learning to swim. And since my tail was still in hiding and bridge debris marred the waters, it was all I had.

This was not the way I'd intended to start my day. But at least the aggressive new pool-owner (because there was no way in hell I was going back in) had jolted me awake. I wouldn't need coffee today, which was a good thing because I'd drunk way too much of it lately.

Two hours later, I gripped my second mug of coffee like a lifeline in the cafe, staring at the empty tables with a heavy stone settling into my stomach. The table in the far corner, where Walter used to frequent, was particularly unnerving. We hadn't seen him in a month.

We hadn't seen much of anyone since the bridge collapsed, supernatural or otherwise. Even the regulars from Treater's Way kept their distance. I was unable to find my tail again. Bridge House was giving me the silent treatment. Only Aunt Ruth seemed unaffected by our sudden disconnection. She awoke every morning and hummed her way to Illusion Square to talk to her tree.

I envied the simplicity of her life and, not for the first time, wondered whether it was faith in me or old-fashioned senility.

Frankly, I would have taken a dose of either these days.

"There you are. I thought you'd be in the pool again." Iris crossed the porch in a long, yellow sundress that flowed as she moved. She pulled out the chair next to mine and lowered into it with the grace of a gazelle.

I'd stopped comparing my athletic and simple vibe to her consistent glamor, but I couldn't stop the tug I gave my basic black athletic shorts, as if they might turn into an evening gown if I pulled hard enough.

"Can't swim in the pool." I whipped my hair into a quick ponytail with the holder I kept around my wrist. It was nearing ten, and the mid-August heat drenched me in sweat the moment I walked outside. "There's a killer bug in it."

"A what now?" I opened my phone to show her the picture I'd managed to snap from a distance in the half-second it had gone still. She dropped her head back to laugh. "That's just a toe-biter, Misty."

I stared at the image, suppressing a violent shudder. "Then why was it headed for my face? Seemed like it wanted to pinch my eyes out."

"You need to drink less coffee." Iris lowered my mug to the table with a chuckle. "It's a water bug. They'll nip at anything. Too small to cause more than a little prick."

"No, thank you, I've had enough of little pricks." I scratched the back of my neck, where a thousand imaginary insects wriggled through my ponytail.

"When are you going to let me fix that for you?" Iris jabbed her finger at my ponytail as if it had committed a heinous crime. "You haven't had a cut or style since you moved here."

I was saved from answering by Kitty, who emerged from the kitchen with a breakfast burrito in one hand and tea in the other. She set the tea in front of Iris, her usually sardonic expression muted. I stared at the burrito. I hadn't asked for it, but now that I saw it, I realized it was exactly what I wanted this morning.

"Kitty? How do you always know exactly what food I'm craving?"

"You always want the same thing. Coffee and a burrito."

I dismissed the casual jab, even as I started to fret that I had become uber-predictable. Underneath the angst was a small thrill, though. I had a regular order and a routine. My cheeks burned from the happy jolt in my heart, in such sharp contrast to the sadness across Kitty's.

"Sure, but you knew everyone's orders. You know ..."—I gestured broadly—"back when we had customers." I'd meant it in farce, but I regretted it when Kitty blinked sudden tears away. "Sorry. I'm a dolt."

Both she and Sam arrived each day on time and prepped for a day of cooking and serving. I couldn't pay them, and they'd dismissed me the moment I'd brought it up. Sam told me being there was their purpose, and they aimed to fulfill it. But as time wore on and all of our efforts to restore what we'd lost failed, they'd become shadows of themselves.

I must have made a dozen phone calls to the New Orleans Department of Transportation. Same with Treater's Way. North Bridge was low on their list. A road to nowhere straddling two worlds. Even my attempts to call in favors from contacts I'd met through Daniel resulted in faux-sympathy and a promise to "look into it" once hurricane season was over.

By then, we'd be dead in the water. And Lucas, who had yet to show his face since he'd threatened me and destroyed the bridge, would own the island. I had no doubt once everything was in his power, North Bridge would suddenly become a priority, and Bridge House would once more thrive.

The supernatural would return. The waystation would be restored. And Lucas would decide which paranormal beings reached their full potential and which wouldn't.

My lone bite of burrito turned sour in my mouth. I struggled to swallow it, pushing the plate away.

"Kitty?" She turned to face me, twirling her single lackluster ponytail in one hand. I missed her three vivid tails. "What happens to you and Sam if I ... you know ...."

I looked to Iris for help. "Wet the bed? Screw the pooch?" She lifted one side of her mouth. "Lay an egg?"

I had a disturbing flash of my mother as a full mermaid, her stomach large with child. Would a mermaid be able to swim pregnant? Did their tails swell the way my ankles had with my daughter? As I'd neared my due date, I couldn't even wear shoes. Not that I could reach my feet to put them on, but—

"Misty?" Iris snapped her fingers in front of my eyes, jerking me back to reality.

"Sorry." I shook my head to clear the image. "Do you know if mermaids lay eggs?" Two bemused sets of eyes bored into me. I lifted my shoulders in a shrug. "I can't help where my mind goes sometimes."

Iris, who was far more used to my shenanigans, shook her head and returned her attention to her tea. Kitty held my stare until I fidgeted in my seat. She heaved a sigh and removed her apron, pulling a chair from the neighboring table to join us. Dragging my plate toward her, she bit into my burrito and chewed.

My jaw dropped. I'd never seen Kitty eat. I rarely saw her sit still.

"Mmm." She swallowed and laid a napkin over the plate. "I see why you like these." She propped her hands under her chin and rested her elbows on the table. Up close, tiny lines around her eyes and thinning lips hinted at her true age.

"I'm Kitsune, Misty. A messenger. Bridge House called me here, just as it's called all of us. My purpose is to serve those who come seeking their path. Sam's purpose is to provide the nourishment they need to travel their road."

She rose and re-tied her apron then cleared the table of dishes. "If you fail, we will follow our purpose as long as Lucas allows us to." She twirled on one foot, headed toward the kitchen. "But we won't be happy about it."

I reached out one hand and pressed it against the worn planks of Bridge House, longing for the connection I'd rejected when I'd first come back. I wished more than anything for Walter the Lincoln impersonator's knowing gaze on me.

The weight of my looming defeat dragged my shoulders away from my ears. Sweat pooled at the base of my spine and trickled down my neck. I yanked my ponytail off my skin in a fit of frustration.

"Are you painting any of the rooms today?" Iris's voice was uncharacteristically soft. "I only have one appointment this afternoon. I could help." I stared at the empty table, rather than meet her eyes and see the compassion laced in her voice reflected there.

I had planned to paint upstairs, and clean debris in the backyard. Each day, I'd done as much as I could while my contractor Buford and his small team made slow progress with the tools they could hand-carry.

But the thought of going up the stairs and facing another dreary day filled my legs with lead.

"No." I loosened my hair, inspecting the split ends, grateful there was no gray. Yet. "If you only have one appointment this afternoon, could you do something about this?"

Iris clapped her hands and hauled me from the chair. She kept her grip firm on my wrist as she all but ran to South Bridge. I didn't know what was about to happen, to my hair or to the island.

But at least, when I failed, I'd look good. Probably.

CHAPTER 2

*I*ris chatted and sang while she worked on my hair, refusing me access to a mirror until she was done. It was her effort to keep me cheered up, and I had to admit it was working. By the time she twirled me in my seat and whisked the cape away, I was grinning from ear to ear.

The grin faltered when I finally got to look at what she'd done, but it didn't fade. Hair that used to hang mid-back stopped just above my shoulders in a blunt bob that framed my face. She hadn't changed my color, but she'd added all this cool movement and layers that somehow made it look healthier. Even though she'd cut it shorter, it *felt* longer, and complemented my features. My eyes were somehow wider, my lips fuller, my cheekbones sharper.

The last time I'd felt this beautiful, I was in the water with Norbert, free and fully in my mermaid form. It was easier, in the water, not to worry about whether your nose was too large or care about the slight paunch that would never leave a lower belly after birth. It didn't matter when the world around you had less structure and expectation.

Being yourself on land? That was a real challenge. I met her eyes through the mirror, the shimmer of my tears reflecting the mystical rainbow that surrounded her. "You're a goddess, Iris."

Iris snorted, a sound very un-goddesslike. "No kidding." She brushed a stray hair off my back with a lip that quivered. "Seemed like time you embraced your human side, too."

It had been easy the past month to forget the call of my siren song and the inner urge that lured me to leave this world behind and let my mermaid-half take charge. Since the night the bridge was destroyed, I hadn't heard it. I'd assumed that, like everything else on the island, my tenuous connection to the magic had snapped.

But with Iris's words, I realized it had quieted because it was winning. Sitting in a salon chair and enjoying the way my new do left my shoulders a touch bare put me back in touch with my humanity. And once the cord re-tied itself, my siren song wailed, filling my ears until I couldn't hear the world around me.

"What is it?" Iris's brows crinkled as she studied my face. "What happened?"

"Nothing." I closed my eyes and pressed my tongue to the back of my throat in an effort to still the melody now coursing through me. "I was just thinking how lucky I am that we've rekindled our friendship."

I lifted out of the chair and pulled her into a hug, wiping tears from my eyes as we separated. "I never had a friend like you in New Orleans, Iris. Sometimes, I wonder if it would have made a difference."

"I'm glad you didn't," she whispered. "It's why you came back to us."

I took my time on the way back toward Illusion Square and the forest that led to South Bridge. I hadn't spent much time in Treater's Way since I went to school here, and while it had changed in the most mundane of ways—updated signs and repaved roads—the core of it was the same. Very few businesses lined the roads, and those that did were mostly essentials like the post office and a convenience store.

My stomach clenched as I wandered past the bank. I had no doubt Lucas was in there, but I was in no rush to confront him. Since he'd taken his full form and Norbert had bitten his weird cow tail off, he'd kept to himself. While that didn't exactly comfort me, it did give me hope that he was still licking his wounds.

After all, with the bridge collapsed and only a few weeks left until our agreement expired, he had only to bide his time and wait for me to fail.

Most of the activity still centered around Illusion Square and the big box store across the parking lot that stood out like a sore thumb. Aunt Ruth was in her usual perch near the Mighty Oak. As I approached her, a small gust of wind lifted the leaves of the tree, and they whistled as if complimenting me. Ruth clapped her hinds like an excited toddler. "Look at those fancy locks!"

I let out an awkward giggle, unable to resist the desire to run my hand through my hair. "Yeah, I finally let Iris work her magic." I joined Ruth on the bench surrounding the tree's trunk, admiring the gilded compass at the base. "What's your friend saying today?"

"She says that you're beginning to lose hope." Ruth patted her hands on the bark. "And that she wishes you understood."

I peered up into the tree, its canopy so thick it blocked out the sun, creating the sensation that the oak grew up into the sky and above the clouds. Deep grooves shaped like claws adorned a branch midway, reminding me there were whispers of a dragon that lived nearby. Two months ago, I would have dismissed the rumor. I knew better now.

"What is it you want me to understand?" I'd never spoken to the tree before. As far as I knew, only Aunt Ruth did. But I directed my question to the trunk, my voice little more than a broken whisper.

"That you're the connection." The voice that answered wasn't the trees, which was a good thing. I might have lost it entirely if the tree spoke. I snapped my head toward the woman standing before us, who had somehow snuck up while I was staring at branches. Marilena owned Thrive, the gardening boutique in the corner. We'd met briefly when I last visited Illusion Square but never had a true conversation.

"Huh?" I scrunched my eyebrows together as if seeing her more clearly would help me understand what she'd said.

"You're the connection." Her smile held a wisdom that suggested she was on the other side of something I was still trudging through. Up close, it hit me that she'd been part of Daniel's circle once upon a time.

I could see it in her now, that hint of the posh and glamor of being married to one of the most prominent surgeons in the city underneath her casual comfort. And my heart beat a bit differently as I remembered Daniel and I attending a fundraiser where her charming, handsome husband drank too much champagne and berated her in front of the crowd.

"You're the connection, Misty." There was no longer a ring on her finger, not even the faded lines of one. And serenity soothed the lines of her face. She handed me an iced latte with a wink. As our fingers touched, a spark zapped through me, the electricity of magic touching magic. "Not the bridge. Not the house. Not the water. You."

With a kiss to Ruth's cheek, she strode toward her shop as if she hadn't shifted my world.

I sipped the coffee with shaking hands, waiting until Ruth was ready to return to the island, pretending the entire time I wasn't quivering inside. Ugly little whispers of guilt quieted my siren song, telling me I should be back at the house making phone calls or polishing furniture.

But I was tired of taking my tiny hammer to the massive iceberg of problems on the island. And while I could admit that something about her words rang true, frustration made my lips curl. If I was the connection, why couldn't I feel it?

Every day I spoke to the house and wandered to the remains of the bridge to try and latch onto the last remnants of power that

I hoped might be floating amongst the debris. I walked the shores and meandered the forest, whispering to the dirt like magic was a four-leaf clover I just had to find.

Sure, I still had my doubts about my ability to be the island's caretaker, but those were ingrained in my human side. No matter how far I'd come since I caught Daniel cheating, the years of his not-so-subtle jabs at me created an imprint on my heart that I hadn't quite shed.

I could already tell what it meant to be a mermaid; I'd had a taste of it. And I had confidence that if someone came to the cafe and wanted to know how to embrace their true self, I'd be able to guide them ...

I snorted out loud, earning a mild grin from Ruth as she hummed alongside me.

I was kidding myself.

Until I chose which world I wanted to embrace, I couldn't help anyone else. No matter how much I wanted to. Even if the house was restored, it would not fulfill my purpose until *I* was restored, too.

I wouldn't get my connection back until I'd made my own choice.

And the island knew it.

CHAPTER 3

A few of the men in Buford's crew had taken up residence in the one bedroom they'd managed to finish. As we approached the porch, they chatted over beers, playing lively music and laughing over shared experiences. The sounds of their mirth met us as soon as we'd crossed the bridge, but while Ruth headed to greet them, I paused and scanned the shore.

Norbert was not in his usual spot on the rocks. The sun wouldn't set for another hour, and this would be his usual prime spot to grab the last of the rays. I sent the porch crew a wave and headed over to the rocks to get a closer look. Shielding my eyes, I searched the water for his bumps and found nothing.

My heart did a little jump as I realized I hadn't seen him in days. We'd stopped our morning picnics with him so I could work on the house before heat overcame our ability to work outside safely. By evening, I was too exhausted from the physical labor and the phone calls begging the city to help me that I'd fall into bed and pass out.

"Norbert?" I followed the shore to North Bridge, calling his name as if he were a lost dog. Moldy planks rose and fell with the soft waves, and the charred stench of burning wood still hung over the water like a fetid reminder of destruction.

Night overtook the sun, stealing my vision of the water. Norbert's nest wasn't far from here, but there was no sign of movement from that direction. Panic rose from my core and flooded me, turning my skin hot. What if he was hurt? What if he'd been forced to leave? What if Lucas had done something to him?

That fear was enough to lift my siren's song. She woke like a beast, screaming her melody so loud in my ear I clamped my hands over them. My head clamored with it. The only way I would find him is if I used my tail. There was no question; I was going in.

I gripped the hem of my shirt and lifted it over my head.

"Misty! He's safe. It's okay."

I yanked my shirt down, squeaking like a frightened mouse. Dimitri trotted toward me, the lights from his house forming a silhouette around him. Now that I'd seen his full troll form, I couldn't unsee it, and it hovered like a mischievous shadow.

He slowed his steps as he approached, angling his head as if I had two of them. I punched his shoulder with the force of ten pieces of paper.

"You scared the hell out of me." It was getting darker, as were his eyes, their golden glow deepening into thick honey with an intensity that skittered my heart into my throat. "What?"

"Your hair." The words were little more than a grunt, and I found myself unable to do more than stare back at him, the sounds of the bay and night and unseen creatures in the nearby forest fading away.

A slap hit the water, the thunder of power, breaking our gaze. Norbert hovered at the edge of the shore with a gator's grin, his black eyes full of mischief. "Am I interrupting?"

"Norbert!" I dropped to the sand, my stomach still in full roller coaster mode. "I was about to go in and look for you. Are you okay?"

"I'm glad you didn't. It would have messed up your pretty, new 'do."

"Oh. Iris did it. She didn't want me to spend the day sulking and painting." I tucked my hair behind my ear and shook my head. All this fuss over a haircut? I didn't want to think about what a hot mess I must have been when I got to the island. The idea made my cheeks burn hot. "But that's not important. Tell me where you've been."

"He's hiding in a cove behind my house." Dimitri jerked his thumb toward the worn-looking shack he called home. I squinted beyond the building, wondering how there was room for anything before the bayou fed into the swamp. Dimitri's eyebrows knitted together in a scowl. "It's bigger than it looks."

The gruffness of his earlier voice was gone, and the mild irritation I was used to replaced it. It calmed me down, as if knowing he was annoyed with me put us on even ground. Norbert still hovered at the edge of the water, so I turned my attention back to him. "Why are you hiding?"

"Lucas has been skulking around." Norbert turned in the water, snapping at something unseen. A long, narrow outline slithered away.

"Snake!" I lurched backwards, landing flat on my butt in the sand and pushing with my palms to get as far away from the shore as possible. When my back hit the edge of the clearing, I yelped like a puppy whose tail had met a boot and rolled onto my knees. It was only hearing Norbert's chuckle that returned me to my senses.

I rose as gracefully as I could muster, dusting myself off and standing tall. Dimitri lifted one eyebrow at me, his expression suggesting he was considering calling a professional to check on my mental health. I shrugged, brushing invisible sand off my shoulder. "I'm jumpy. A bug attacked me in the pool this morning."

Dimitri didn't bother to hide his laugh. "A bug?"

"A big bug." I held my hands three feet apart, indicating the shape of that little creature in my overtired, anxious mind. "And that's not the point. There was a snake in the water, and it tried to grab Norbert just now." I ping-ponged my glance between them. "Am I the only one who saw that?"

"He's sending them after me." Norbert braced his front legs and crawled onto the sand. "I don't have many predators, but some snakes can wrap themselves around me. I guess he figures a snake looks the most like the tail I took from him. If he knew I'd kept it, he'd send something bigger." Norbert chuckled to himself. "It sure looks pretty in my nest."

I did not bother to hide my full-body shudder. There was a bloody tail-stump in Norbert's nest. And snakes in the water I had almost dived into a few minutes earlier. "I'll take my chances with the toe-biter."

"Why are you swimming in the pool when you're a mermaid?" I plopped down next to Norbert, scanning the water as I mumbled my response. "What was that?" he asked.

"Because my back hurts." My cheeks burned so red I dropped my eyes to the ground. I could practically feel Dimitri's confused stare on the back of my neck. "I'm almost fifty. When I was in mermaid form, my body ached." I plucked an errant strand of dead grass and fiddled with it. "And I haven't been able to find my tail, so I figured the pool was a safe way to ... practice being a mermaid."

"It'll come back, Misty. Give it time." Norbert tapped the edge of his snout to the side of my leg, and I dropped a hand to his head. Things were dire, but having an alligator familiar was about the coolest thing that had ever happened to me.

"My ankles." Dimitri extended his hand, lifting me to my feet. "When I shift into full form, my ankles throb for days." I smiled his way, letting his awkward expression of solidarity jitter about inside me. "You should get back to the house. He's not shown up in full form yet, but I wouldn't put it past him."

He peered toward a rustle in the top of a tree, as if discussing Lucas had brought him into existence. I kneeled down to Norbert to touch my forehead to him. "I'll come back with marshmallows."

"I'll walk you to the house." Dimitri's hand hovered mid-waist, as if he might put it at my back or hold my hand. He stared at it like it had lifted of its own accord.

Norbert chuckled and slid into the water. I watched until he disappeared behind Dimitri's house. We followed the shoreline, rather than risk walking through the woods, my heart thudding in my chest. Part of me braced myself for Lucas to come storming out of the trees a hundred feet tall with a face twisted with wrath and a bandaged backside.

The silence between us was louder than any scream I could imagine. Dimitri walked stiff as a statue, his fists clenched at his sides and a vein near his jaw ticking like a time bomb. Heat radiated off him in waves that seemed to burn my skin.

I'd seen him this angry before on my first night at the island. He and Lucas were mid-fight when he'd sent Lucas flying across my bumper. I didn't fully understand his anger now, but my instinct was to soothe it away.

I rubbed one hand along his upper arm, suppressing my physical reaction to the bicep flexed under my palm.

"It's not really his way."

Dimitri halted his steps to face me. "What?"

"Lucas. He's the sneaky type. He's got long-term plans that make his image important. To rule his own mini empire that includes the town with all the magic and the island that makes magic stronger." I gestured toward Bridge House, just visible above the levee, the fairy lights I'd found so magical pitch black.

"What's your point?"

"He's not going to crash through the island in full Hulk and squash me like a bug." I started up the levee barely managing to suppress the shiver the visual brought me.

"It's not his way," I repeated as we reached the porch. A dim light cast a shadow across Dimitri's face, hiding his expression. "Maybe he's licking his wounds right now, but more likely he's planning a way to get out of our agreement and force us out of the house."

It hadn't occurred to me until I'd said it aloud. I rubbed my hands along my arms, now covered in hundreds of goosebumps. Dimitri's silent nod of agreement did nothing to soothe my fears. He looked down and kicked at an invisible bump.

"You were going in."

"What?"

"The water. When I found you on the shore to let you know I was hiding Norbert, you were about to swim."

"Oh." I tugged at the bottom of my shirt, wondering how much he'd seen before he approached. It was a blank spot in my head, as if it happened a year ago and not an hour. Which direction had I been facing? Did he see more than a sliver of stomach? Not that it mattered, he'd walked in on me mid-transformation before when I'd had no pants on at all. If that hadn't sent him running—

"... tail?"

"Huh?" Dammit, I'd done the thing where I wasn't listening again. I squeezed my eyes shut and opened them wide, trying to bring him into focus. "Sorry, I zoned out."

Dimitri chuckled. "I said, does that mean you've found your tail?"

He stepped forward, just enough for me to see the hope in his eyes, and a nugget of lead settled into my stomach. He wasn't asking if I'd found my tail. He was asking if I'd connected to the magic again. He was asking if I was going to save the island.

"Maybe?" I swallowed down the lump in my throat, lifting my shoulders and dropping them down with a sigh. "My siren song yelled at me earlier. It was the first time I'd heard it in weeks."

He pressed his lips together, covering his disappointment by trotting down the patio steps. When he reached the bottom, he turned to me. "It's a start, Misty. Keep at it, we all believe in you."

I wasn't sure that was true. I wasn't sure I believed in myself anymore. "Be careful."

"Yeah. You, too."

I stayed on the porch until Dimitri disappeared in the shadows along the walk to North Bridge. I stayed longer, peering toward Norbert's usual perch on the rocks, just visible in the rising moonlight, unable to shake the feeling that I would never see him again.

CHAPTER 4

The hold music was a symphony rendition of "In-A-Gadda-Da-Vida" that made me want to rip my ears off. It had played on repeat for the past forty-five minutes. At first, the tune was a delightful surprise, an alternative to Yacht Rock that I appreciated. But after three-quarters of an hour of repetitive violin screeches I didn't want to be in this garden anymore.

The only reprieve was that Buford and his micro-crew had stopped whatever work they were doing upstairs. For a while, the banging of their hammers had been in sync with the faux-cello synthesizer until I felt lost in a drug-fueled sixties haze.

"He's almost ready for you, hon. Sit tight." The same chipper, southern voice I'd spoken to every weekday for the past month quipped into my ear. "Okay, he's ready, I'm going to put you on hold then transfer you."

"In-A-Gadda-Da-Vida" resumed, followed by a click, followed by a dial tone. I planted my face on my pillow and let out a long, throat-scorching scream.

I had to hand it to the New Orleans Department of Transportation ... they had a sense of humor.

I sat up, ready to call back, when Buford belched from the

doorway. He rarely cleared his throat or said "excuse me" to get attention. It was always gas.

He fiddled his filthy ballcap in one hand, and an excited little smile played on his lips. "Ms. Misty, sorry to interrupt, but we have something to show you. Can you come upstairs?"

I sunk my phone into my pocket, grabbing a third cup of coffee on the way.

"We can't finish the exterior, not yet. We need a lifting machine and that'll have to wait for the, uh, well, you know." He had a spring in his step as he all but danced up the stairs, and a welcome grin lifted my cheeks. Whatever he was excited about, it was adorable. "But it's real good progress, and if you can talk to the house again about the wallpaper …"

He drifted off as he reached the door to my mother's old bedroom, swinging it open with a graceful flourish that belied his large frame. I inched past him and into the room I one day hoped would be mine. What I saw left me breathless. My hands clutched themselves at my chest to keep my heart from exploding with joy.

The floors were pristine, the wide wooden planks smooth and finished. Someone had polished the armoire. They had reupholstered the reading chair. The bed still lacked a mattress, but it was cleaned and ready.

I turned in a circle, my arms extending like Maria in *The Sound of Music*. Even my siren song hummed at the sensation of home this room brought. I ran to Buford and lifted to my toes to plant a noisy kiss on his cheek. "Buford, this is amazing."

He blushed beet red, returning his cap to his head. "All the bedrooms are ready. We still have a few finishing touches, but we figure once you get the bridge fixed you can open them up and start taking a few guests who might not mind that the outside still looks like it weathered a storm."

"Because it did." I ran my hand along the hideous pink blossoms, still wilted on the walls. Through the sheen of my tears, a few of them bloomed. A spark rippled through my palm. The hint of our connection. The house, like me, trying to fight its way out of dormancy.

"There's more." Buford crossed the room to the white-washed balcony doors, opening them to the view of the bay and, far in the distance, the dome-topped skylight of New Orleans, made blurry by my tears. Sunlight sparkled off the water, as if glitter filled the air, and I stepped out and gripped the railing.

I had a balcony. I had my dream balcony.

A small round table of peacock blue and a white bistro chair nestled into one corner, painting the picture of mornings where I took my coffee here before heading down to the shore to chat with Norbert and have breakfast with Iris, greeting guests and visiting with patrons of the cafe along the way.

I snapped a selfie, sending it to Charley with an all-caps text I knew she'd razz me about. I didn't care. The rush of hope inside me was new and wonderful, something I had only begun to experience when Lucas destroyed the bridge.

But now, I had a balcony. I could picture my life as the Queen of Bridge House. I had space for guests. A cafe in working order. A dedicated construction crew. A best friend. A loving aunt. And a potential ... something.

All I had to do was build a bridge. How hard could it be?

Iris crossed from the south, sending me a wave as she strolled toward the house, sea-foam greens billowing out from her dress. I saluted back to her. When I squinted my eyes, I could just see the hint of a rainbow trailing behind her. It wasn't as hard as it used to be, to see the magic underneath the mundane. Maybe, if I tried that more often, I could reclaim my connection to it.

As I was heading downstairs, my phone chimed. I checked the text, expecting a snarky response from my daughter.

I stopped dead in my tracks before my foot hit the bottom stair.

My husband's name scrolled across my screen.

CHAPTER 5

> Misty, it's Daniel. I'd like to schedule a time to
> meet with you.

*I*t's Daniel. As if I didn't know the number. As if I'd
deleted his contact in a fit of rage. As if removing his
name would remove a lifetime of history.

The truth was far different. The truth was I'd barely thought
about him. Except for the occasional late-night Google search to
gratify myself that a scandal was heating up for him and his new
girlfriend, I was surprised to find he no longer held real estate in
my mind.

We hadn't spoken in months, not since I found him in bed
with another woman. Rumors of his affair had circulated for a
while. But with us still technically married and me missing from
the New Orleans social circle, he was facing hot water.

Besides which, she was probably beginning to show. He
wouldn't be able to hide the fact he'd gotten another woman
pregnant much longer.

I didn't feel an ounce of sympathy, and deep down I'd

expected a phone call eventually. This limbo wasn't good for either of us.

But that didn't mean I had to feel good about it.

> I'm happy to drive to Bridge House if that is more convenient.

The second text brought red to the edges of my vision. He was expecting an immediate response, watching his phone for confirmation I'd read the message, replying to let me know he was waiting. A passive-aggressive game I hadn't played in so long that the trigger to reply, to placate his demands, caught me off guard.

Coffee soured on my tongue. Hell no. My old life would not take up the space I was creating in my new one. I didn't need his silent judgment here, not when things were hanging in such precarious balance.

He didn't even know the bridge had collapsed. He hadn't bothered to check on me until he needed something. I stopped outside to stare up at the balcony I hadn't noticed them building.

My friends had done that for me, because I had friends. And family. And sure, I needed money and resources and had no idea how to get them but ...

It hit me then, a bolt of lightning from nowhere, a flash of inspiration so obvious I was ashamed it hadn't struck me sooner. I needed money and connections and resources to fight Lucas and win back the house.

And the man who had them needed a divorce from me. And was waiting for me to text about a meeting. This would be the one time he couldn't let me down because saying no to me would mean putting his career in jeopardy.

Facing my past could create the future the island needed if I played it smart. I sent a fast reply.

> Yes, it's time that we had a discussion. But I
> will come to you. I'll send you some dates and
> times in about an hour.

I watched for the telltale sign of three dots. They hovered, faded, and hovered again. Finally, my response lit with a thumbs-up reaction.

CHAPTER 6

A jagged but defined orange border lined the edge of Daniel's hands, clasped tight on the table in front of him. He'd had lung cancer, so I understood why he might be avoiding the sun, but someone needed to guide him on the proper way to use spray tan.

That someone would not be me.

His salt and pepper hair was longer than he used to keep it, though it tapered at the edges toward his ears and along his neck. It was a good look for him, somewhat Kennedy-esque, which I imagine was what he was going for, given he had a Marilyn now.

I swallowed down the bitterness that rose and held his eyes. Their color always appealed to me, the way green swam with blue, reminding me of water. Despite the fake tan, his skin glowed from regular facials, and he had a nice square jaw and full lips.

But I'd known this man for twenty-five years. I recognized the strain beneath the polish. While I'd been disconnected from the world at Bridge House, he was taking a beating here in New Orleans. I didn't mind the savage sliver of glee that wormed its way through me.

He and Lucas were cut from the same cloth. Their focus was power, and they molded themselves to anything that would aid in that goal. Haircuts and fake tans were superficial, and for the first time I recognized that Daniel was devoid of any true depth. I couldn't believe I'd let myself wade into such shallow waters.

I snorted at my dad pun, and he lifted one manicured eyebrow in question. I shook my head. We were on opposite ends of a polished mahogany conference table, our lawyers perched beside us discussing terms and conditions. Or something. I wasn't listening because I had no interest in negotiation. I'd called my father's lawyer because I didn't need a shark. For the first time in my life, I had power and a clear direction forward.

It was exhilarating.

The lawyers both grew quiet, so I knew some agreement had been made. I glanced at the papers laid out in front of me, covering up my gasp with a cough. "That much?"

"You've earned it." Daniel's cold smile spread his lips thin. "You cared for me when I was at my most ill, Misty. You raised our stunning daughter, and you provided a beautiful home. I don't think it's inaccurate to say that I would not have won my reelection if it weren't for you."

He reached across the table to place his hand on mine, and I steeled myself to keep from removing it. "I owe you an apology. It must have been humiliating to find me ... well, to walk in on such an unpleasant surprise."

His tone oozed sincerity, but it stopped short of his eyes. He'd been told by his political advisors, or his lawyer, or some other person on his team to apologize to me. Because they perceived me the way he did.

Meek. Compliant. Accommodating.

Fuck that.

I tilted my head and mocked his tone. "Unpleasant is one word, Daniel. I can think of a few others. Shocking. Devastating." I crinkled my nose. "Smelly."

Both he and his lawyer shifted in their seats. His lawyer adjusted the perfect knot of his tie. It was all I needed to tell me I had wiggle room to get what I wanted.

"Did you know I have photos?"

He had the decency to lose his confident air, but only for a second. I drank it in.

"You know, when I walked in on you and Dawn, her legs up in the air, you pounding into her, I snapped a picture. I had my phone up, if you remember, because I'd gotten a message from Charley that she was settled into her dorm. It was an emotional moment." I fixed him with a glare. "It's why I came home early, because I needed comfort from my husband."

I paused for effect, taking the glass in front of me and enjoying a slow sip. "I didn't know why I took a picture at the time—it was certainly never my intent to create bad publicity for you—merely an instinct, I suppose. And you kept my phone."

I tapped two fingers on the paper. This was a complete bluff, easily disproved, but some instinct I didn't understand spurred me on. "Imagine my surprise when I synced the new phone Pop bought me." I held his gaze a moment longer, then shifted it toward his lawyer. "All of my pictures. Uploaded to that cloud thing."

His lawyer leaned in, as if to whisper in his ear, but Daniel waved him away. An air of malice crossed his eyes, sending my heart into a thump as adrenaline coursed. But I held firm, even as his smile faded. "What is it you want, Misty?"

"In addition to this?" I tapped the papers again. "Do you have any connections in the transportation department?"

His brow furrowed. Whatever it was he'd expected, probably more money, this surprised him. "I have several."

"And the title office for Bridge House? That's under the Treater's Way purview. Do you have contacts there?"

"It is." He reached for the papers, but I pressed my hand to them.

"This is under the table, Daniel. Let's call it a gentlemen's agreement. I don't want anyone to know about it until it happens."

His lawyer gripped Daniel's arm, but he waved the man away

as if he were no more than a fly. "How do you know you can trust me?"

I couldn't help it. I laughed. He was right. The illusion of a man I could trust had been shattered months ago.

"Let's just say I'm trusting my gut, not your word. Still, we can settle everything today. Right now, in fact."

He pressed his lips together, a longstanding tell that he was considering. A spark of hope flitted across my belly. "A quiet divorce?"

"A quiet divorce," I said, nodding to my lawyer in agreement. "I'll wait for the papers to be drawn and sign them as soon as the rest of it is done. We both leave here with what we want."

"And your pictures?"

My lips curved up. "What pictures?"

For a moment, the lawyers and the room faded away, and Daniel looked more like he had in college. Maybe it was because I was fighting back, or maybe it was his excitement at the prospect of a deal. We were on even footing, and I was grateful to look at him, even for a moment, and see the man I'd married rather than the man he'd become.

I was grateful to be able to tell that man goodbye.

Daniel lifted his chin an inch, the most subtle of nods, but I knew I'd won. His lawyer stacked the papers on the table, leaving the room without another word. My lawyer followed.

"Do you think you can handle Bridge House on your own?" Daniel extracted his phone from his pocket.

"I'm not alone." My smile widened. "But absolutely."

He heaved a sigh, opening his phone with one swipe. "Who am I calling, and what do you want?"

I reached into my purse and pulled out a pad of paper and a small box. I fingered the box for a moment, stepping on the desire to open it and admire the contents one last time. On the paper, I wrote my short list of demands. I placed the box on top of it and slid it across the table.

"Make those things happen, please. And keep my wedding

ring." A lump caught in my throat, making my voice waver. "I know it was your mother's. That's something you should hold on to."

Daniel swallowed, and I was more than a bit surprised at the tears that welled. "I wasn't going to ask for it back. I thought ..." He let his voice trail.

"You thought I would be vindictive and keep it or push for more if you brought it up. So you were going to let it go."

The smile that crossed Daniel's face was real, and more than a bit bittersweet. "I didn't know you at all, did I Misty?"

"That's not your fault," I told him. "I didn't know me either."

CHAPTER 7

*T*wo hours later, I had everything I wanted and was officially divorced. As I walked to the parking lot, I rubbed at the strange, hollow spot between my chest. It was as if I'd been floating between two different worlds for months, focused on one while ignoring the other, and both were about to collide.

What I'd just done was more than a little reckless. Several pieces had to fit together, and at the right times, for my plan to work. I had no idea how much political power Lucas had, or how upset he would be when he learned I beat him at his own game. But it was the only play I had left.

I drove toward Treater's Way in a daze as the sky darkened around me, tapping one finger to the steering wheel in tune with the music quieting the part of my mind prone to chatter. While the loaner Dimitri had given me was nice, and definitely more comfortable than Old Bessie, I missed the familiarity of my college Jeep. I'd hung onto it against Daniel's protests. A reliable but imperfect reminder of who I was before I met him.

One day, I would drive it across North Bridge again and find myself able to enter the city without trepidation. As the random thought slammed into me, I veered off the main road and pulled up to the battered entrance to North Bridge. The city had not even bothered with a warning sign or a barrier, and the signal indicating it was safe to pass still flashed green.

I guess they assumed it was obvious the bridge wasn't there anymore. Yet here I was thinking of times I would cross it again. My siren song uncoiled within me, whimpering at how near I was to water, at how thoughts of human activities still came so naturally to me.

Because, as it turned out, I was much better at being human than I'd given myself credit for. Daniel's casual line at the lawyer's office skittered across my mind, turning my thoughts black. How dare he imply I wasn't capable of running the bed and breakfast?! I'd managed to keep his campaign afloat when he was diagnosed with cancer. I'd organized his fundraising parties and tended to him after chemo.

Hell, I'd changed his pants a time or two when he was too sick to get out of bed. And I'd run the house while raising our daughter through teen angst. Then, I'd seen her off to college, where she thrived.

All the things a mother does. All the things a good wife does. And yet, when he looked at me he saw someone incapable. Because I'd been meek.

The raw truth of it gutted me. I'd put my entire life on hold, cooking the foods he wanted and devoting myself to taking care of him. And while his lack of gratitude stung, his betrayal was an even deeper slap across my face.

But the worst part was how, in my pursuit of keeping everyone around me taken care of, I'd forgotten about myself. Looking back, I realized I'd given him no reason to view me as strong, because I'd acted weak. And everything that might have brought me joy—cooking, swimming, friendships—were placed so far on the back burner they'd dried out and become crispy remnants of what they once were.

But in the past few months, I'd tended to them again. I'd helped them start to sprout little seedlings of joy. And they'd taken on a different meaning. No one on Bridge Island questioned my ability to run the B&B. Nor had they asked me about being a mermaid.

They'd never questioned either. The only one putting pressure on me to choose between the worlds was ... me. I was the one still in the headspace that I couldn't do more than one thing. That I couldn't be good at more than one thing. Despite the fact that, my entire life, I'd managed to wear several hats, I still wasn't giving myself credit for everything I balanced.

I ran my hand along my thigh. With enough concentration, I could make out the soft, rippling scales underneath my skin. Underneath my favorite pair of athletic shorts was magic and beauty.

I was beautiful, both the human and mermaid parts of me. Not unlike the way we'd been repairing the house, one little piece at a time working with what we could carry, all the parts of me created one picture that was Misty.

I didn't want to leave Bridge House. I wanted to continue to cook—when Sam allowed me to—and open the bed and breakfast to bring more help to more people. To watch them flourish and blossom and grow, just as I was doing. I didn't want to leave my daughter and miss her becoming the strong and capable woman I knew art school would produce. I liked my life on land.

And, just like the bridge and the house would be, I was made from sturdy construction, from parts that were once broken now made whole.

But I didn't want to abandon the call of the water, either. The sensation of coursing through water, of the cool waves traveling across my skin as I soared in the air and dove down deep, was exhilarating. Being able to see the layers of invisible life below the surface—beyond where the fish swim near the shoreline—was a gift I treasured. My song would not lure sailors to their doom but would call those in need.

I could call them to Bridge House, where we'd help them discover their magical abilities, see them develop and grow over time. I could embrace the water when it yearned for me, dive in when I yearned for it. I refused to lose this new, feminine, and powerful part of me.

And, just like my mermaid mother, I had parts of me that were daring and adventurous and brave.

All those pieces. Being a mother. Being a business owner. Being my own person. Being a mermaid.

They were all parts of one whole. They weren't separate pieces, though. They weaved together.

My mother had to choose. Aunt Ruth had to choose. But I didn't. I couldn't.

I couldn't choose because to turn my back on one would destroy the other. Instead, I had to find a way to embrace each of them, interwoven as they were. I had to make them connect.

And just like that, Marilena's words from the Mighty Oak made complete and total sense. *You're the connection, Misty.* I hopped out of the car and approached the bridge, squinting like I did when I wanted to see Iris or Dimitri's magical forms.

And there was North Bridge. The mystical outline of its power shone gold like Dimitri's eyes. Gold like the treasures of the world. A gold so brilliant it reflected onto the water, leaving a shimmer that called to me.

Rummaging through the trunk, I found two old plastic grocery bags. I removed my clothes, wrapping them around my phone and tying it all together, hoping it would stay dry but not caring as much as I expected myself to.

My song rose within me, no longer a scream. A happy melody, complex and lovely. I peered over the embankment to the water below. As if he'd heard it, Norbert flicked his tail in the water. I gave him a wave, tying the bag around my waist.

There was no doubt I'd find my tail when I needed it. I dove off the broken edge of North Bridge.

CHAPTER 8

$\mathcal{I}$t was fully dark when I reached the other side, so I took a moment on the shore to let myself dry before extracting my clothes from the grocery bag I'd carried with me. It had done the job, for which I was grateful. I did not want to show up on Dimitri's doorstep sopping wet and naked. At least not tonight.

I stayed in mermaid form while the moonlight rose, testing the strength of my song. It beckoned, there was no doubt it would always beckon, but the song had shifted. Instead of a pull, something I felt I had no choice but to gravitate towards, it was an invitation. An open door to the open sea.

"You look different." Beside me, Norbert's eyes scanned the trees.

"It's probably the hair." I patted him before giving him a nudge that did nothing to move his massive body. "Go back to your hiding space, friend. I've got this."

Once he'd disappeared back into the water, my tail shifted with my will. I pulled my clothes on and hopped to my feet, rubbing my stomach as the sensation of my mermaid curling up for a nap filled it. I wasn't worried. I'd wake her when I needed to.

The edge of the embankment was above me, Dimitri's

ramshackle cabin to my left. It nestled between the broken pillars of the bridge. When the bridge was intact, it would not be visible at all. Did that bother him? To have the thing he'd rejected keep him protected all these years? Did he miss it now that he was exposed?

The cabin was pitch black, and for a moment my confidence faltered. I'd assumed he'd be home, and if I waited until he was, I wasn't sure I could say what I needed to. What if he was on a date in town? I'd never seen him with another person but surely the man dated.

Or maybe he just didn't like light. He was a troll.

I followed the long edge of the cabin toward the open waters. A smaller, second building I'd never noticed before was lit from within, and the familiar tunes of Steely Dan drifted on the light breeze playing off the water.

I headed toward the sound, stopping short as I came closer to the open garage door. It had looked tiny from the outside, but the building stretched at least twenty feet back. A long wall of the concrete building displayed an impressively organized array of tools and baskets with printed labels. A ceiling fan slowly shifted the air, wafting the subtle tang of gasoline towards me.

I neared a car I'd never seen before, jacked up in the center of the room, and wedged my foot to kick the familiar worn boots sticking out from underneath. Then I paused. Dimitri may not respond well to me inviting myself into his ... magical troll house. I'd seen his true form before. I did not want to be on the bad side of it.

"Dimitri."

His toe tapped to the music, but he didn't stop working.

"Dimitri."

I repeated his name a few times, gave up, and kicked his boot.

"What the hell?" Dimitri's roller cart slid toward me, and I backed away as he leapt to his feet, wrench in hand.

I lifted my hands in front of me in self-defense. "Don't swing! It's just Misty."

"Why would that stop me from swinging?" Dimitri glared, his hand squeezing the handle of the wrench as if he were considering throwing it at me. "Please stop kicking my feet." He dropped the wrench to the ground, where it clattered over the music, which he shut off with a curse. "I hit my head every time." He rubbed his forehead, leaving a streak of oil.

"I said your name this time. Five times." I grabbed a shop towel from a labeled box on the table, approaching him and wiping his forehead. "Sorry about that. I needed to talk to you."

"It couldn't wait until tomorrow?" His breath tickled my forearm, and I realized just how close to him I was standing. He smelled like motor oil and cedar-wood, a scent I hadn't realized had become so familiar to me. With a clearing of my throat, I backed away.

"No, actually. We need to talk tonight." It was quiet in the garage, too quiet. "Please."

He sighed, swiping the cloth from my hand to wipe his fingers. "Let's go inside."

"Hey, I have a question." I followed him outside and toward the cabin. He flung open the door and flipped a switch on his right. "How do you get cars down here? I mean ..."

My words died on my lips. Just like the smaller building, this cabin was bigger on the inside. It wasn't just big, though, it was clean and trendy. The open concept living and kitchen area were decorated in forest greens, with aqua blue accents in the form of sleek picture frames and throw pillows carefully arranged on the long, leather couch.

Light gray wooden floors ran toward the back of the cabin, where there were several doors. I wandered toward the wall-mounted television, stopping at the entertainment center below it, where I picked up a picture.

A woman with flowing, brunette hair and bright brown eyes smiled at the camera. She wore a sunny yellow dress that nipped at her waist and flared down the skirt, where two little boys clung to her legs. One of them had sandy brown hair, carelessly dropping into his wide, golden eyes. He frowned toward the camera, his lips at full pout. On her other side, a slightly taller boy with dark hair and a similar smile had one hand lifted in a wave. His smile stirred me, as it was the most pure and joyful I'd ever seen, and it was familiar even though I'd only seen it a few times.

"So you do know how to be happy."

He took the picture from my hand, setting it face down on the surface and handing me a beer. "That was the last summer we were all happy."

"Lucas didn't look happy."

"I don't think he's ever been happy. Well, once for a short while."

I turned to face him. "When he was with Iris?"

Dimitri's eyebrows lifted up his forehead. "You know about that?"

"She mentioned it in passing, once. And when Lucas lost his cool and destroyed the bridge, well, she grieved." I sat on the opposite end of the couch and waited until he was comfortable. When I had his attention, I swung my arm to encompass the room. "So ... magic cabin under a bridge?"

He chuckled. "I am a troll."

"You're a troll. I'm a mermaid. Iris is a goddess. No matter how many times I hear it, I'm still not completely used to it." I took a swig and looked around. "Does this troll magic extend to North Bridge?"

"It should have." He leaned back on the couch and crossed one leg. He'd removed his shoes and left them by the door. "I had a connection to it, just a slight one, but now that it's destroyed, I can barely feel it."

"I get it. The same thing has happened with me and the house. Well, until about an hour ago."

He brought his bottle to his lips. "What happened an hour ago?"

I took a shaky breath. My idea, so clear before, suddenly silly now that I had to say it out loud. What if he rejected me?

"I got a divorce. I'm officially single."

A million emotions crossed his face. Wariness, sympathy, and confusion marred his features. He gave a long, slow swallow. My heart hammered in my chest.

"I'm not here to seduce you, Dimitri."

"I didn't think you were." I pursed my lips at him. "Okay, the thought crossed my mind."

"Uh-huh." I finished the beer and set it on one of the coasters on the glass table in front of me. The man had coasters. And they weren't the flimsy kind you pick up from a bar or Gino's Pizzeria. They were stone, with etched fleur-de-lis. "You're an enigma."

"What do you mean?"

"The coasters." His bland stare told me he had no idea what I was talking about. I shook it off. "Never mind. What do you know about my ex-husband?" It was such a strange sensation, to say ex. I was surprised I didn't stumble over the word.

Dimitri scratched his jaw. "Politician type. Decent amount of power. Family money." He looked at me over the edge of his bottle. "I gotta say, Misty, he doesn't seem like your type."

I wanted to explore that. I was curious what my type was or how he saw me, but this was not the time for that. "He used to be my type," I said. "What else do you know?"

He gazed at me without answering, and though I didn't want to squirm, a rush of sensation filled my stomach. "It's okay, Dimitri. You can be honest."

After a long, painful pause, he sighed. "The rumor is you caught him cheating, and now his side piece sleeps in your bed and is carrying his baby."

I mimicked an arrow to my heart. "Ouch."

"Sorry. I don't do subtle."

"Nope. You definitely don't do subtle." I swallowed down the shot to my pride, hoping one day it would sting less. "Well, in addition to all of that, which is correct, he has connections. And because his reputation is far more important than I am, I had him in a corner when it came to divorce proceedings." I lifted an unused coaster and twiddled it in my hands. "And today, I got a divorce."

I let the statement hang in the air, hoping he would understand me without my spelling it out. After a moment, he leaned forward, and his gold eyes sparkled, as if a match was lit inside him. For a moment, I saw a hint of the magic he kept dormant within, then mischief replaced it.

"You got enough money to pay off the lien against Bridge House."

"Oh, I got more than that." I smirked. This was more fun than I'd anticipated. "You still on our side?"

He propped his hands on his knees, setting the bottle on the table with a loud clunk. "I'm still on your side."

"Good. Then don't tell your brother that by the end of the day tomorrow he will have zero hold on Bridge House. Or me."

Dimitri dipped his head, and for a moment my heart stopped. What if my instincts had been wrong? But his shoulders sagged in relief, and when he lifted his head, his eyes shimmered. "He'll make a play for North Bridge. It'll be the only bid for power."

"Oh, about that." I had to admit I was going to enjoy this part. "Let's say that, hypothetically, you had a mermaid, a goddess, and an alligator willing to help you rebuild the bridge. And a construction crew." He opened his mouth to speak, and I held up my hand with a grin. "And what if the gang at Illusion Square helped us."

That spark lit again, but he thinned his lips in worry. "It's a start, Misty, but we still have a resource issue. And a permit one."

"That's where this gets fun." I planted my feet on the ground and leaned forward. "It seems that today, the New Orleans Department of Transportation recognized the urgent safety issue the residents of Treater's Way face with North Bridge demolished. In an unprecedented show of efficiency, they managed to gather the materials needed and they will be delivered by end of day tomorrow."

I rose from the table, collecting our bottles and wandering to the pristine kitchen to throw them away, marveling at the sleek stainless appliances and stone blue backsplash. He was standing by the picture of his mother when I returned. I cleared my throat to get his attention.

"You should know that I've decided not to choose. I'm going to live as a mermaid and a human and embrace my role at Bridge House."

The shift in his expression warmed me from the inside. An admiration I hadn't expected twitched his lips into a smile that he quickly tamed. "Your mother tried that."

"It's not the same. She never *wanted* to do both, not really. I do." I walked to the front door, the footsteps behind me telling me he'd followed me outside. The moon had risen overhead, but darkness filled the small walkway. Still, his eyes shone. "I have the permits in-hand, and tomorrow morning I'm going to see your brother at the bank. On his turf, I'm facing him down."

My throat clogged, but I swallowed down the rise of fear. He wouldn't turn full troll in the middle of the city and smush me. Probably. "Tomorrow evening, I'm gathering all the help I can find, magical and mundane, and rebuilding North Bridge. I'm going to restore Bridge Island."

My heart stammered in my chest. I took his hand, lacing his fingers in mine and holding them between us, meeting his eyes full-on. I needed him to see how serious I was and to understand that what I was about to say to him wasn't coming from a place of cruelty. I needed him in a hundred different ways.

"But if you don't do your part, Dimitri, and claim your right as the troll of North Bridge, Lucas can sweep it all away from us."

His body jolted, as if I'd hit him, but I held firm to his hand. Then his head inched forward, bringing our lips closer together, the gold of his eyes swirling like lava. Everything inside me tingled; my core did somersaults. My tongue darted out, running along my lips as if I could already taste him.

This was not what I'd come for. Not at all. I didn't mind it one bit.

Time held as we stood frozen, statues eternally on the brink of completion. I could have stood there forever, locked in that anticipation.

But there was a tiny sliver of doubt within me, and now that I was back on the island and finally in the right headspace, the house reached for me. This had to wait. And I had to know he would do his part. When I spoke, my voice was little more than a whisper.

"Dimitri, please tell me you're ready."

He didn't answer, but he released our hands and stepped inside, turning his back to me as he closed the door.

CHAPTER 9

*D*espite the tension of the day and the near-miss of hotness, I slept like I didn't have a care in the world. In the bedroom I'd coveted since I was a little girl. My bed felt as if it rolled on soft waves, the perfect level of darkness kept me rested, and the complete absence of regular house creaks and groans meant I didn't wake one time.

When I finally opened my eyes, after a long stretch, I headed toward the balcony. And stopped mid-step. The wallpaper was gone. In its place was the soothing shade of sea blue I'd envisioned what seemed like a lifetime ago.

"Thank you." Tears filled my eyes, and I touched my forehead to the wall. The familiar hum of the house vibrated through me. My voice was a whisper.

The vibration grew, as if the house laughed in delight, and a thought that wasn't mine flooded my brain. *Just this room.* I laughed with it.

"Just this room. For now."

The energy was everywhere. The construction crew bellowed from the second floor as they polished newly built shelves to a shine. Aunt Ruth was nowhere to be found on the ground floor, but the earthy scent of her lingered in the gleaming parlor.

Sam and Kitty stood close in the kitchen, secret smiles on their faces and delight in their eyes. Kitty held a go-cup of coffee out to me, which I nearly dropped as Sam wrapped me in a bear hug.

"Damnedest thing." His loud voice echoed in the kitchen. "The back burner on the stove's been giving me fits for ages. This morning"—he released me, laughing when I stumbled backwards —"it popped right on."

"Isn't that something?" My cheeks already ached from smiling, but I couldn't seem to stop it from spreading. "You guys up for a project tonight?"

I found Buford and discussed my plan with him, then trotted to South Bridge to find Iris. Norbert still wasn't on his perch on the shore. I could swim out and find him later if I needed to. My siren song tittered at the thought.

Iris rocked in a bright fuschia rocking chair on her porch, her hair looped into a bun on her head, and a housecoat more glamorous than anything I'd owned in a long time tied at her waist. She held her palm out to me when I approached.

"No one sees me without makeup."

I slammed my hands over my eyes with a huff. "You have five minutes. I have places to go and people to see today."

"I'm already done."

I removed my hand, and Iris stood in front of me, hair coiffed and makeup impeccable. A laugh escaped me. "Man, I just got a tail."

She looped her arm around mine with a chuckle and led me to the porch. Unlike Dimitri's rundown exterior, Iris's cabin was more like a country cottage than a setting for the final scene in a horror movie. I peeked in the window, unsurprised to find that it was huge and ritzy inside, with gold fixtures and vivid colors. "This island never ceases to amaze me."

Iris crossed her legs as she resumed her perch on the chair, gesturing to the one beside her. "It is indeed a special place." She assessed me, stopping with her eyes at the top of my head. "You didn't fix your hair this morning."

"I probably never will, Iris. You'll have to get used to that."

She was quiet for a moment but lifted her chin in a nod. "You look different."

A sudden rush of nerves made my palms clammy. Unlike Dimitri, I was sure that Iris would embrace my surprise plan, but I wasn't sure how she'd adjust to my sneak attack on Lucas. Or that it relied on a man she hated stealing the power Lucas wanted.

"I've figured it all out, Iris. Finally. And the house and I have reconnected. Hell, the whole island and I are connected now."

"Good. Did it let you get rid of the wallpaper?"

"Just in my room," I admitted. We shared a laugh that soothed me enough to continue. "Listen, Iris, Lucas doesn't know it yet but, I've won." I waited, trying to assess the emotions that crossed her face, but her magical makeup was a mask I couldn't read. "I'm rebuilding North Bridge tonight."

Her eyes flooded with tears that, for the first time I could remember, she did not bother to check. They slid down her face and left a trail on her neck. "Lucas will try to claim it."

I drew in a shaky breath. "I've already prepared Dimitri. I'm hoping he'll step up when the time comes." I rushed on, ignoring the sneer his name always brought to her. "But there's nothing I can do about that. My duty is to Bridge House, and the island. I'm the Queen."

I'd hoped the queen mention would make her smile, but her lips stayed pressed together. She looked out toward the bay, her expression indecipherable.

"He wasn't there when his mom died." She gnawed on her lip while tears streamed. "We were at her side. Me, Lucas, and Aunt Ruth were. But the day before she'd asked just to see her sons. Apparently, she told Dimitri he was the right one to claim North Bridge, and she wanted to see it before the end. He refused, and she was crying his name when she died, but he was nowhere to be found." She inspected a manicured nail, searching for flaws that didn't exist. "It tore Lucas up that he was right there, and she couldn't see him because she was searching for Dimitri."

She shifted her body to face me. "He never claimed the bridge, but he never let Lucas have it either. Lucas shut down emotionally after that."

A nasty feeling squeezed at my heart. I'd known Dimitri was a grump and had struggles of his own, but I didn't know he was carrying so much regret. And the sympathy I felt for Lucas was an unwelcome bitterness coating my tongue. He was manipulative and power-hungry, and, when provoked, downright dangerous, but I knew how it felt to be let down by someone you loved. It was an icky, out-of-control kind of ugly I didn't wish on anyone. Even a politician.

Dimitri and I had come very close to crossing a line. And he'd turned away from me, too. Doubt shrouded my confidence. Nothing I planned would work if Dimitri didn't claim the bridge. "I'm sorry I never asked why you hated him."

"I wouldn't have told you," Iris replied. "Not until I was sure you were ready to hear it. Besides, we've been re-learning what our friendship would look like. I just needed you to know before you put all your faith in Dimitri that he might not show up the way you want him to. When he finally came back, it was after their mother's funeral."

I let that sink in. What kept Dimitri from claiming the bridge? Where had he gone? Was it really just grief and time, or was there a bigger reason he hadn't told me? I couldn't know. And at the end of the day, I couldn't do anything about it.

"Iris, if I've only learned one thing since I returned to the island, it's that I cannot control it all. What I *can* do is show up fully and take the next step, or swim, forward." I pulled her into an awkward sideways hug. "You're my best friend. I'm sorry he hurt you."

I hopped to my feet, wincing when the rocker swung with too much force and banged against the cabin wall.

"I can't control North Bridge, but both Lucas and Dimitri

need it to be restored. I think, or I hope, that Lucas would rather have a shot at power than let it all collapse. I guess I'll find out tonight. Are you with me?"

When Iris lifted herself from the rocker, her housecoat dissolved into an elaborate dress of pure rainbow. She was taller than me in her human form, but as the goddess she towered so high she had to duck to keep from slamming her head into the overhang. I squinted at the brilliance of her power, shaking my head.

"I just got a tail."

"You're a freaking mermaid," the Goddess of Rainbows told me. "And a damn good human." We fist bumped, her hand twice the size of mine. "I'm with you."

Assured I had at least one more person in my corner, I crossed South Bridge to Treater's Way and the showdown with Lucas that would decide my future.

CHAPTER 10

$\mathcal{I}$ planned to stop at Illusion Square on the way home for Aunt Ruth and to ask The Eight (even though I still didn't understand that) if they would help us rebuild the bridge. I exited the forest, and Marilena lounged outside her store. She gave a brusk nod that filled me with electricity. As I scanned the Square, I realized that each of the shop owners stood guard by their signs. The Mighty Oak rustled its leaves in greeting, and Aunt Ruth saluted me with a mischievous grin. Somehow, word had already spread. I just hoped it hadn't reached Lucas.

He didn't feign a pleasant exterior when I entered his office, and a solitaire game still reflected from his monitor onto the window pane behind him, just like when I'd first entered with Ruth. I had to wonder if he actually did any business here in Treater's Way, or if he was just waiting around to gain control of Bridge Island.

A few flyers were strewn across a filing cabinet on my left, all for New Orleans politicians. Daniel's grinning headshot peeked out. I pointed toward them. "Are you taking notes on a successful political run, Lucas?"

He had the good sense to blush, the red of it underscoring the lackluster sheen on his hair. He rose with a wince, bracing himself on the edge of the desk as he stood, and limped to the flyers to shove them in the trash. Damnit. There went my guilt again.

"I'm sorry that Norbert bit your tail off."

"Are you?" The hateful glare Lucas shot me would have caused me to cower not two months ago. My pulse was still doing jumping jacks on my wrist. I didn't think he would move into his troll form and squeeze me until my head popped off. But you never know. "Perhaps you should not have encouraged him to come after me then, Misty."

I crossed my legs in a casual gesture. I had leverage he didn't know about yet, but I wasn't going to be cocky about it. Even if I wanted to. "He's my familiar, and you were going to kill me. I'm not sure what else you would expect from a magical being in the form of a gator."

The hate in his gaze faded, just a touch, and he settled himself back into his chair. He opened a drawer near his side and pulled out a manila folder, clasping his hands on it and facing me. "I lost my temper."

"That's one way to word it. After all, your fiendish plan to control Bridge House for political power over the paranormal kind of falls to pieces if no one can get to it. I know you didn't intend to destroy the bridge that night. Did you know the magic would go dormant when you cut it off from the world?"

His swallow was audible, telling me he hadn't. I'd assumed his quiet over the past few weeks, and his sneaky attempts to hurt Norbert, were focused on the tail. But from the distress building at the corners of his eyes, it was clear he'd messed up even worse than he'd intended.

Good.

I pasted a cordial smile on my face and waited as he worked to recover.

"Yes, well, I've always been sensitive about my brother betraying me." He opened the folder and slid a sheet of paper towards me. "I have to say, it's impressive that you were able to get him to choose a side. He's infamously neutral. You must be even more charming than I thought."

I read the title of the paper, my mouth turning to cotton. *Voluntary Repossession.* "What's this?"

"It's what it says, Misty." He tapped the title, his voice oozing with condescension that slimed over me. I was going to have to take a shower after this. "You and I had an agreement. It is one week until that agreement comes due, and you have not rebuilt Bridge House or shown in any way that would give us faith that you will be able to repay the lien.

"Despite the unfortunate events that destroyed North Bridge, I assume that's why you're here. To admit defeat or beg for more time that I will never give you." The finger he used to tap the title dragged along the desk. He lifted it and caressed the line at the bottom, a smug smile on his face. "I don't technically need your signature, Misty. But I want it."

Until this moment, I'd been confident in my path forward from the second Daniel and I had reached our agreement. There were moments of doubt—whether Dimitri would still choose my side, how Iris would respond—but I'd been sure this part would go my way.

The desire to please, to cower, lifted unbidden inside me. My lifelong instinct to doubt and question jumped up and down. What if the paperwork I'd seen yesterday was fake? What if Daniel had called the bank after I left and called it off? What if there was some legal loophole I hadn't thought about? What if—

"...need a pen?"

"Huh?"

Lucas's triumphant gaze filled my vision.

"I said, do you need a pen?"

I clamped down on the rush of anxiety making my skin hot and my eyes blur and shoved the paper back towards him.

"I don't need a pen, Lucas. I came to ask you to confirm on that computer that you only play games with that you received the wire transfer I sent through yesterday." I leaned forward. "I'm here to take ownership of Bridge House, once and for all."

The nails on his hands grew. It was the only sign I had that I might be in trouble. His fingers trembled with a tension that made his veins bulge through the sleeves of his dress shirt. He wet his lips. "I beg your pardon?"

"Yesterday, when I was finalizing my divorce with Daniel, a wire transfer was sent through paying off Aunt Ruth's loan." I leaned back and re-crossed my legs. "A second set of papers was transmitted that transferred the title of Bridge House to me."

His expression shifted from confidence to disbelief in the blink of an eye. In any other situation, I might have laughed at how comically slowly Lucas swiveled in his chair to face his computer. He tapped a few keys, and I watched the reflection in the window behind him as he moved a card from one pile to another in his game. "Unfortunately, Misty, it does not look like it was received. So if you'll just sign the papers—"

"That's okay!" I brightened my voice and clapped my hands together. "I have the confirmation numbers on my phone." I swiped the screen to show him with a savage sliver of glee. "You might want to think about redecorating your office. You know, so your screen doesn't reflect on your pretty, wide windows."

I was on my feet before he turned. Once he knew I'd won there was no telling whether or not he'd be able to contain the troll. I didn't want to find out. "I'll assume your boss has the papers ready for me, anyway. That's what he told my ex husband yesterday."

I spun on one heel and headed toward the door labeled Bank President. Inside was a portly man with a handlebar mustache I'd never seen before. Lucas belted my name before I reached the door, and the man looked up. Recognition passed across his face, and he lifted a folder from a tray beside him.

Relief made my knees buckle. Everything had gone through after all.

"Misty," Lucas yelled again when I didn't acknowledge him.

The other patrons of the bank eyed him curiously. He'd ripped his fingers through his hair, leaving it mussed and untidy. His eyes were wild with rage.

He yanked my arm to spin me around, bringing his mouth close to my ear, his voice little more than a growl. "You may have the island, but you'll never get that bridge rebuilt. I will make damn sure of it."

Lucas losing his temper was not something I wished to revisit, and I didn't want to show my hand completely just yet. If he didn't know we were rebuilding the bridge, he couldn't stop us. A deep fury boiled in him, radiating like a heat that burned my skin.

I looked around, hoping he would follow my gaze. Lucas's boss had risen to take my side, and people outside the bank stopped to peer inside. Everyone was paying attention to us.

Lucas was losing his grip on his reputation, and that would not be something he could come back from.

Somehow, it was far more dangerous than a giant Huldrekall, crashing towards me in the dead of night, intent on my destruction.

I disengaged his claw like fingers from my forearm. Deep purple welts remained. "You've lost, Lucas. Don't make it worse."

As if coming out of a trance, he glanced around us, to the security guard cautiously approaching, to the older woman clutching her hand at her throat, to the young child cowering behind their mother.

He stood tall, straightening his hair with one shaky hand. He plastered a smile on his face that looked like a grimace and shoved his hands in his pocket as he left.

CHAPTER 11

$\mathscr{I}$ couldn't help but laugh as I saw Iris headed toward me. It was a natural laugh, but even to my ears there was a shrill tension in it. I'd been sitting on the newly finished porch steps for an hour, waiting for the sun to set and pretending that I was enjoying an evening break while I waited for Ruth.

But Ruth had come and gone. She was now inside, no doubt reclining with her feet up, enjoying whatever book she brought home from Illusion Square. Occasionally, I'd walk to the edge of the drive and back, just to make sure that Norbert was still sunning on the rocks. He'd lift one eye toward me, as if to acknowledge my presence, then he'd shut it.

But his tail flicked in a way that told me he was as nervous as I was. Maybe he didn't really want to bite anyone.

"What are you laughing at?"

"You," I said. "But don't take it personally. It's not because you're funny looking. It's because I've never seen you look so casual before."

"Well, I figured this would make the most sense for major construction." She'd pulled her hair into a tight braid behind her back and was wearing a faded pair of denim overalls that stopped short mid-thigh. Any Catholic school back in town would have sent her home for the day. A tight red bandana was wrapped around her forehead, and although she'd kept makeup on, she wore a decidedly masculine pair of steel toed boots.

I shuffled my feet as she settled on the stair opposite me. "Is it there?"

"I think so," I replied. "There was a bit of mayhem, and more than a bit of clatter, about an hour ago. But I can't see it from here so it's hard to tell. I'm still not sure how they got it across the water. Buford and the crew are already down there."

"Dimitri didn't tell you how it was going?"

"If that was all arriving, I imagine he would be pretty busy."

"He could've texted."

That hadn't occurred to me. I didn't even know Dimitri's phone number. If something was going terribly wrong down there, I had no way of knowing. Lucas could have found a way to bypass the delivery of materials. My nerves shot into my throat, and for one split second I was positive I was going to vomit. I stood and began to pace. "We should just go down there so I can get this over with."

Iris patted the stair beside her. "Just have a seat. We'll know when the time is right."

I wrung my fingers together and sat next to her. "Thanks for doing this with me, Iris. I know it's a complicated situation for you."

Her sigh was heavy. "This is right. The rest, well, chicks before dicks."

I laughed so hard I choked on my spit. "I've never heard that one before," I said between coughs.

Her lips curved up in a mischievous grin. "It's my version of hoes before bros. I don't slut shame."

"Fair enough." I bumped her shoulder, and we fell silent as the sun set over the water.

The gang from Illusion Square cleared the forest and South Bridge not long after. Marilena sent me a wave as they marched toward the North Bridge path. I squeezed my eyes closed to steady my breath, wishing my heart would stop training for a marathon.

We went to the levee first to check on Norbert. He was no longer on his rock, and a thin ripple of water followed his wake as he swam away from the shore. I had to hope he was on his way to the bridge, but I scanned for snakes just in case.

We followed the shore toward the bridge, where a hum of activity had already begun. Large lights cleared a path through the trees. Buford directed our skeleton construction crew, giving instructions over the tinny music blasting from a tiny radio. Dimitri's radio.

He stood near the site inspecting blueprints in a black t-shirt stretched taut across his chest, and I breathed a sigh of relief when I saw him. At least he was helping. It was better than him disappearing. Yellow tape roped off most of the upper levee and the road that led from North Bridge to Bridge House. On one side were the thick, tall piles that would replace the broken ones jutting from the water. Next to it were wooden slats.

There would be more steps, more to do once Dimitri claimed the bridge, but this was the first.

He tipped his hardhat to me when I approached. "Turns out all the supplies had been cut and measured when an inspector deemed the bridge unfit for travel some time back. Only Lucas's palm greasing held them off, and they'd sat in storage ever since. No wonder you got everything so quickly."

Fresh anger bolstered my nerves. We were doing this. Rip parts of the old out, replace them with new. Easy. A bulldozer roared to life, bringing fresh nerves to the surface. "How did they get a bulldozer here?"

Dimitri cupped a hand to my shoulder. "I carried it."

Fear and relief waged war within me, and his touch burned my skin from the inside. He pulled my arm close to inspect the finger-shaped bruises along my forearm. His breath grew ragged. His eyes darkened. His words were a growl that brought goose bumps to my flesh.

"Did he do this?"

"He lost control at the bank, but it was brief and he recovered." I dropped my voice low so others wouldn't hear. "He'll come tonight, Dimitri." I wanted to say more, to say something magical that might seal the deal and ensure he did his part. I came up blank.

He'd walked away from his mother on her deathbed. I had no reason to believe he'd come through now. But the savage anger, raw on his face, gave me hope. "I'm putting my faith in you, Dimitri."

Something I couldn't read swam in the gold of his eyes. "I know it."

With a nod, I stepped away to visit with Buford and get the plan. He chatted with Iris, a grin covering his face when he saw me. "We're getting a hell of a lot of overtime pay tonight!" I let the laughter bubbling up in my chest surface. It popped some of the tension I was holding. "Are you ready to get going?"

"Not yet. I have to, you know ..." I looked helplessly at Iris who simply lifted an eyebrow to me. "Don't you know?"

Dimitri had approached, and at my stuttering he scowled and crossed his arms. "We don't know, Misty, so whatever it is you're feeling weird about, just go ahead and spit it out."

Iris snorted. "Such a troll."

"Let's not start that." I put my hand between them, as if they might throw punches. My nerves were already frayed; I had no room for their ridiculous banter. "I have to transition. Don't you?"

"Oh." Dimitri's scowl lightened slightly. "Yes, but I guess it's not that big of a deal to me."

"Or me," Iris put in.

"How nice for both of you, that you've transitioned your entire life, and it's not a big deal. Meanwhile I've had about two months of experience with this, so I still feel a little awkward. Gee, I hope that's okay."

"Don't be so dramatic." Dimitri waved his hand. "Just get on with it."

"I have to change first."

Dimitri sighed as if I told him I had to write a dissertation before we could begin and had not started doing the research. "Do you want to use my bedroom?"

Heat at the back of my neck flared and ran up to my earlobes. "No, I can just go by the side of the garage."

Once I was behind the building, I made sure no one above could see me and shrugged out of my clothes. A soft lapping at the water told me Norbert was behind me. "Don't be a peeping gator."

"Do you think you're funny?"

"A little." Naked, I took a moment to settle my breath. I couldn't fight the sensation that once I slipped into the water, I would be helpless if Lucas launched an attack. "Have you seen any snakes?"

"Don't worry about them." Norbert slapped the water with his tail, as if snakes that could kill an alligator were not a big deal. "Get on with it. We have a bridge to build."

I waded in further, until I felt the familiar tingle of my tail rising, then I cut through the water like a knife through butter and swam to the side of the bridge, staying underwater up to my shoulders.

Dimitri and Iris waited on the shore. "Show us your tail already." Iris shouted.

On a whim, I grinned, dove into the water, and flipped into the air, sending my tail into what I thought was a beautiful shimmer in the moonlight. But I misjudged the distance, and the water slapped me in the face. As I landed flat on my back and went under, I remembered that I was also topless. So much for grace.

When I rose to the surface, Iris was doubled over with laughter, and Dimitri's lips were pressed thin. "You can laugh."

Dimitri coughed into his hand, then shook his head. "I guess it's my turn."

"Go ahead." I splashed water in his direction. "Bet you can't make it as cool as mine was."

Dimitri grinned, then turned and took two steps.

By the third step, I could feel the rumble from the ground beneath the water. His body elongated. The ground shook. HIs clothes were on one minute, then ripped away from him the next as his thighs grew as thick as the tree trunks that barely reached his round, perfect ass.

I swam a bit closer to get a better look. The black of his hair was gone, the gold of his eyes had spread. He was a bronzed, muscled statue from head to toe. His arms were bulging biceps and round shoulders. His stomach was lean and defined. And as he kneeled on one knee to see me, his absurdly large penis swung to the ground.

I gulped. That was something I could not unsee.

"For God's sake." Iris rushed forward to put her hands in front of my eyes. "Can't you put that thing away? We want to repair the bridge, not batter what's left of it to pulp."

He shook his head and waved his hands, and a pair of golden briefs covered him.

"Could have done that in the first place," she grumbled.

"Your turn, prude." Dimitri's voice didn't sound like his anymore. It rumbled and was deeper.

Iris twirled in a circle, letting her rainbow spread around her like wings. When she'd shown me her true form, she'd tapped it down. But now, in a series of flourishes and jazz hands, she shot up as tall as Dimitri. She flipped her braid, smacking Dimitri in the face with it, leaving a trail of glitter across his gold.

A pang of jealousy flicked through me, surprising me. They would make a good couple, at least in their true forms. Dimitri could run and be free with Iris or do whatever it was giant half-humans did. Meanwhile, I'd be confined to the water. I shook my head of it, remembering some of the wonders I'd seen when I first swam with Norbert. Going far was nice, but sometimes going deep was where the beauty lay.

Buford lumbered over, his neck craning at the two giants. I swam to shore, covering my chest with one hand. I was going to have to figure out a way to be a mermaid in front of people, but oddly I felt more uneasy about my tail than my breasts.

"Woah. I've seen a lot in Treater's Way, but I gotta admit this takes the cake." Buford inched closer, watching Norbert out of the corner of his eye. "The crew is ready. I guess those two will do most of the heavy lifting?"

"We hope to make the work go faster, yes. They'll manage above the water, Norbert and I below. But none of us has experience, so we'll need your crew's help to do it right. Oh, and it's Dimitri's bridge, so anything he wants or asks for, he gets."

Buford nodded. "Not gonna say no to him. Or him." He gestured toward Norbert, pacing the water behind me.

"Norbert's here for protection, but he won't hurt anyone on our side." I reached out of the water to pat Buford's belly. "He won't eat you, pal." When he relaxed, I leaned back. "Any sign of trouble, you and your guys back away and let the big guns handle it. Got it?"

"Got it. But we got permits, so I don't see where trouble comes in."

I blinked at Buford, momentarily shocked by his naïveté. "Yes, this is all legal, but we're doing this at night to get it done fast. Before Lucas can stop us."

His eyes widened. "You guys are going to finish the whole bridge tonight?"

"No, just the part connected to Treater's Way. On the New Orleans side, they are blocking it off and starting their part tomorrow."

"So"—Buford stood tall, hooking his thumbs in his pocket —"I guess you're stuck on the island a little while longer, huh?"

I laughed and flipped my tail. "Not technically. But I couldn't be happier to be here. Now, tell us where to begin."

It took an hour or so, but eventually we found a rhythm. Iris served as communication between us. I swam down to the bottom to pull out the piles, surprised at the strength that I found, and Dimitri lifted them out. He put the new ones in place and tapped them with his fist until they drove deep.

The construction crew followed with a boat to guide us, marking where the new ones went and doing other construction things I didn't understand. The Illusion Square crew, that to my surprise included another mermaid, all had jobs of their own.

Fresh slats were laid along the suspension, and Buford and his crew sawed, nailed, and secured. Each time I stopped to look at it, the outline of its magic remained. It was like we were filling in spaces that already existed.

Someone changed the music to a local band whose peppy songs seemed to bely the dangerous undercurrent of our activity. Before long, there was as much laughter as there was communication.

I hadn't trained enough with my tail, and I was feeling the effects of the fatigue. I pushed until I couldn't, stopping to drink water and have a snack after a few hours. Dimitri knelt to see me.

"I can't get over how big you are." I shook my head, immediately realizing how that sounded. "I mean tall."

He chuckled and held his hand out to me. "My hand alone is bigger than you now."

"Well, that's reassuring. Please don't crush me."

"I would never." He flicked me softly with one finger, mirth I'd never seen on his face as he glanced toward the bridge. "I can see it, you know. What it's supposed to look like."

"Me, too." His head whipped back to me. "Yesterday, before I came to see you, I realized that once I claimed my true self, and the island, I could see all the magic that was already here, and all the potential. The bridge showed itself to me."

A sheen of tears filled his eyes. "You swam to me. I didn't even think to ask."

My tail swished as if dancing. "Oh, yeah, about that. Your car is at the end of the bridge." I gnawed on my lip a moment, suddenly overwhelmed by his presence. "Sorry about that."

Dimitri, the grumpy old troll who lived under a bridge, flashed a brilliant smile that sent my heart soaring. I sure hoped he would claim his right because I was dangerously close to falling for him.

"My mom once said something to me, Misty, that I'll never forget."

His lips moved with the words, but I didn't hear them. Something wrapped itself around my tail and yanked me back. Just before my head dipped below the surface, Lucas crashed onto the site with a roar that stilled the air.

CHAPTER 12

*M*y ears filled with pressure as I was dragged from the bridge and deep into the water. It was shallow under the bridge, but within a few minutes my jaw hit the rocky bottom, and I was being pulled past the bay. A large snake, a species I didn't recognize, gripped tight to my tail. As I struggled to free it, a second slithered around my neck and pulled taut.

I clawed at the skin, impossibly cold and ungraspable. Black hovered at the edges of my vision, but I could feel booms, like large drums being slammed against the floor in the distance. Lucas and Dimitri fighting. And while I hoped Norbert was helping them, I also knew I wasn't going to survive without him.

One of the Illusion Eight was at my side, Viv, flapping her own tail furiously to catch up with us. She throttled the snake around my neck, digging her fingers between my skin and its body to create breathing room for me. I blinked at her, trying to focus even as panic stripped away my ability to think straight.

A shadow swam past me, the clamping of a jaw rattled my bones, and the remaining half of the snake fighting us went limp. Norbert dove for the one around my tail as I rotated toward it. When it saw the gator, it released me and wrapped itself tight around my familiar.

Underwater, I screeched, my siren song bellowing from my core. Norbert spiraled through the waves we created, which made the snake tighter across his body.

"Tools," I shouted to Viv. "At the construction site."

With a nod, she bolted through the water and back toward the bridge. I followed Norbert, dodging the snake's fangs as it lashed out at me, its tail still weaving a tightrope around my gator.

I had no idea what to do, how I could help Norbert disengage. But I knew I wouldn't let him go down without a fight. I bared my teeth. If he could bite a tail off, I could sink into a snake. Ignoring the shudder rippling through me, I gripped the head and opened my mouth.

Viv was at my side, nudging a saw into my hand like a guardian angel with fins. Thank god. I really didn't want to eat raw snake. Pulling the wriggling beast as tightly as I could, I jammed the saw onto its body, clamping my mouth closed to the coppery blood escaping its body. It twisted and writhed. I sawed like I was trying to cut through a noodle.

But it was enough. Norbert's death roll flung the snake loose, and he clamped down on it before it could recover. Satisfied Norbert could handle the rest, I sped to the surface.

Flashes of light, raw power and magic so bright I shielded my eyes, cut through the night sky. Lucas and Dimitri, in full form, swung at one another, harkening back to my first night crossing the bridge. Dimitri's eyes had a purpose that rendered me speechless. Lucas's mouth foamed, his expression delirious.

Dimitri drove him back towards me, away from the bridge. His jabs were meant to force Lucas to stumble. And though Lucas was taller and more slender, there was a sureness in Dimitri's steps I'd never seen before. Each time his fist made contact, it was like lightning and thunder formed a giant ball of destruction.

Lucas gripped Dimitri's arm, stumbling closer. Dimitri placed his palms against Lucas and shoved, sending him to the water. Dimitri marched forward, spreading his legs and planting his fists on his waist.

"I claim North Bridge. I vow to honor those who wish to cross it, to help them find their purpose, and embrace or reject their gifts as they wish. I promise to honor the magic of Bridge House, and to support the mistress of the house in all her endeavors."

He flicked his gaze to me, a flash of relief softening his face. He lifted his hand, moonlight shooting from his fingertips, and placed them on the edge of the bridge. "North Bridge. South Bridge. Bridge House. They will be complete, Lucas. And they will create a haven for those in need."

The wood we'd laid lit from within. The poles we'd stabilized rattled one at a time as the form of the bridge was illuminated like a gilded runway toward New Orleans. The energy behind his power filled the water, leaving my teeth tingling with its intensity. His eyes zeroed in on Lucas, fierce and golden.

"It is done. I accept my birthright."

The lights disappeared, the sky and the bridge returned to normal, but I still felt the hum of energy, stronger than ever, as if a missing electrical cord had been plugged in. The island was whole, and the song of its completeness filled me and mingled with my siren.

As if Dimitri's strength weakened him, Lucas disappeared under the surface of the water as he shrunk to his human form. His arms flailed, breaking the seal of water before sinking under again. Oh dear. Lucas had lost his magic. And he couldn't swim.

I whipped forward and wrapped my arms underneath his armpits, carrying him to the shore. He crawled onto the sand, sputtering and coughing, fixing me with an intense glare before he rolled to his knees and ran. He disappeared into the forest.

"Want me to chase after him?" Norbert appeared at my side, and I hugged him close.

"Let him run. I don't think he has power any longer." I patted my hands along his rough skin. "You're okay?"

"I'm okay." I'd heard of crocodile tears, but I never expected to see an alligator cry. "You have a nasty bruise on your jaw."

"I'll live." I touched my hand to the tender part of my face, already throbbing. "Let's get back to the crew. We have a bridge to finish."

Dimitri stood in human form next to Iris, speaking to her softly. She nodded in response before punching his shoulder. It might have been a reconciliation, I couldn't tell. Either way it was a start.

I stayed in the water while the crew chatted to one another. When they saw me, they grew silent. Dozens of eyes on me, the mistress or queen or whatever of Bridge Island. A mermaid who lived on land. A human who had a tail.

"Buford, why don't you put that music back on. We have work to do."

I tapped my fingers against the water's surface in tune to the new beat, flicking my tail with a light sense of freedom. I was exhausted, shaking, and ached all over.

Still, I wore a smile.

It was going to be a long night. But when it was over, North Bridge would be repaired, and it belonged to Dimitri.

And I was home.

CHAPTER 13

a unt Ruth sipped her tea then planted a wet kiss on my
cheek. I wrapped my arm around her, the porch swing
creaking softly as we rocked it back and forth.

"As much as I love Illusion Square, I sure do enjoy my
Sundays at Bridge House now that it's so pretty."

"Me too." I dropped my head to her shoulder. She tilted her
head to mine.

"When is the grand opening?"

I chuckled. "We still have a lot of work to do. And I'm still
fighting the house about the wallpaper."

"The House will come around." Ruth giggled her childlike
giggle. "It likes you again."

It did, and in that moment, I felt a warmth that came from
the wood and surrounded us, like a matronly hug.

"I'm thinking we'll be ready by the end of September. I want
us open for Halloween. It feels right."

August was nearly gone, but even so in an hour, it would be
too warm to sit outside, even with the outdoor fans we'd installed
in the breezeway and over the new cafe tables. But no one seemed
to care about the heat. Even on a Sunday morning, the cafe was at
capacity.

Business was growing.

Sam was downright boisterous. And Kitty was complaining that she'd need some help soon.

As the sun rose behind me, I stood and stretched.

"Going for a swim?"

I smiled at Ruth. "Maybe in a little bit. I was going to go say hello to Norbert, and just sit with him for a while."

Ruth nodded in understanding. "I don't think Lucas will come after him again, honey. Or you."

There was a sadness to her voice. It was a sadness I understood, the feeling when someone you thought you knew turned out to be different than you believed.

Sometimes, that could be a wonderful thing. Like Iris or Dimitri. Or even myself.

But the hurt of betrayal never quite leaves; even as you move on from it, the sting remains. Even though Lucas was misguided, conniving, power-hungry, and downright dangerous when he lost control, he still had the same troubled past that brought everyone else to Bridge House. No one had seen him since the night we'd rebuilt the bridge.

But while to me he'd never been more than an enemy, the people I loved grew up with him, and I felt their loss as if it were my own. I blew Aunt Ruth a kiss.

"Maybe one day we can get through to him."

I headed down the driveway. A revving engine stopped me in my tracks. Emerging from the North Bridge road was a shiny red Corvette. It sped toward me, braking inches short of my feet and sending pebbled dust across my legs.

"Oh wow." I trailed my fingers along the hood as Dimitri stepped out. "Look at this beauty. You did a great job."

"Of course I did." He was only slightly nicer since we repaired the bridge, especially since it had taken two days longer than we planned. He'd embraced his power, but underneath it all he was still a surly old troll.

"Here." He tossed the keys at me, and I yelped as they slammed against my knuckles and fell to the ground.

"What are you doing?"

"Take them. The car is yours."

"Nuh-uh." I shook my head. "We had a deal. This is your car now. You fixed it, you fixed my Jeep, and you fixed the bridge. I got the house. Fair is fair."

Dimitri kneeled to retrieve the keys. "What you gave me is worth way more than any car." He dropped them into my palm, folding his hand over mine. "You helped me understand who I was. You helped me embrace that I'm a fixer. And you helped me own the power that my mother always wanted me to own. I don't think I could ever repay you for that."

"I'm so glad," I replied, dropping my eyes from his earnest gaze. "But you did all that on your own."

"I couldn't have done it without you. And even if you don't see it yet, this is more than a car, Misty. You've embraced who you are, too. And part of that means accepting who your mother was, and the choice she made. So, this isn't just a dumb old red car anymore. It's a memory. Maybe one of the only happy ones you have of her."

He squeezed my hand one more time then stepped back, leaving the keys in my palm. "You deserve to keep a little something for yourself."

I blinked at the keys through blurry eyes. Who knew that Dimitri could be such a softy? As I thought of my mother, and the pain of her leaving, it reminded me that for most of my life, I'd relied on the wrong people to stay.

I still wasn't sure about me and Dimitri, or the past that caused him to wait so long to claim North Bridge. But he was right. The car did mean more to me now than when I'd arrived. It represented the few times that my mother and I had connected as people. I might never see her again, or get answers to the questions that I had, but it was time to let go.

If I could forgive Daniel, then I could forgive my mother for her choices. And my father for his.

And part of forgiveness meant embracing who I was, and how I was formed, in part, because of what happened to me. I looked out over the water, the call of it rising in my gut and my legs tingling. Norbert was crawling onto his rocks. I longed for a swim.

But it could wait. I had time. I wiped the mist from my eyes and grinned at Dimitri.

"Want to go for a ride?"

It's almost Halloween and time for the grand re-opening of Bridge House. But Misty's struggling with her new role, and good help is hard to find ... unless it's a charming ghost pirate and a flea-ridden werewolf.

^^^ Scan the code above or click here to start reading the hauntingly funny fourth book *Bridge Over Spooky Water.*

WHEN A CLUMSY DRAGON turns out to be her scorching hot ex, will an independent therapist reignite an old spark or let it smother?

^^^ Scan the code above or click here to claim your copy of *Not Yet Old Flames* and join my newsletter.

ACKNOWLEDGMENTS

At this point it's redundant to thank my Jens.

But a special subset of Jens held my hand in that beautiful cabin far away from the world (but really only a three hour drive, during which I blasted Florence + The Machine and Sia and sang until I was hoarse) and got excited about my pirates and mermaids.

So thanks, Jens, for the gift of unquestioning support. And to my Southwest Jens ... pizza rolls and wangs. Forever.

ABOUT JB LASSALLE

JB (Jen) Lassalle is a writer of low-steam romantic and urban fantasy. She likes strong females, dimensional males, and found family friendships that triumph over nuanced bad guys you love to hate.

Jen is a New Orleans resident. The city, and the surrounding areas, serve as a rich backdrop for a world where magic exists and mystical creatures are not only real, but live among us.

When Jen isn't writing, she's hanging with her family and friends at a local park or coffee shop. She likes working out, which is kind of weird, loves yoga, and plays video games. Of course, she reads.

Jen and her husband have two kids. One is an avid competitive swimmer (which sucks up all their weekend time). The other is a daydreamer like Jen who plays the Mega Man theme on his guitar and kicks around a soccer ball.

Jen isn't great with social media, but you can connect with her below. Or, join her newsletter when you claim your copy of *Not Yet Old Flames,* a second-chance PWF romantic short.

facebook.com/jblassalle

instagram.com/jblassalle

amazon.com/JB-Lassalle/e/B0BFJXP4GC

www.ingramcontent.com/pod-product-compliance
Lightning Source LLC
Chambersburg PA
CBHW032110170626
46808CB00008B/3008